# The Best of
# HAPPY
# ENDINGS™

Illustrated by Tony Hutchings
Written by Jane Carruth

MODERN PUBLISHING
A Division of Unisystems, Inc.
New York, New York 10022

# Hoppity Gets Lost

Hoppity liked riding in Mr. Weasel's old bus. He enjoyed going to the stores with Mommy and Tufty. This morning the line was longer than ever and everyone was carrying their biggest shopping bag. Hoppity wished he had one too.

"Keep tight hold of Tufty," Mommy said, when it was time to get on the bus. "I do hope the big sale at the Department Store hasn't started." Hoppity was too excited to reply. He knew where he wanted to go when he got to the store.

The bus stopped near a huge store. Hoppity gasped when he saw the Woodville Bandsmen. They were blowing trumpets, banging drums, and clashing cymbals.

"I'll join the band when I'm big," Hoppity shouted above the noise. "I'll be a cymbal-clasher!"

"You'll be a good boy," said Mommy sharply. "And stay close to me. We must get to the Shoe Department and start looking for a sale on slippers. It's Daddy's birthday tomorrow."

"We're in luck," Mommy whispered to Hoppity when they were in the Shoe Department. "Everybody else has rushed to the coats." The pretty salesperson brought out all kinds of slippers and Hoppity began to wish Mommy would decide. He looked around for something to do and saw an enormous pair of men's boots on the floor. Hoppity smiled broadly as he stuck his feet into the giant boots. At first Mommy was cross. But when she saw the smile on the salesperson's face, she smiled too.

Mommy got some new handkerchiefs for Hoppity and his brother Bobtail. Then she said, "How about some milk?"

"No thank you," said Hoppity firmly. "I want to go to the toys. So does Tufty. He wants to see all his bear cousins and I told him he could!"

"We'll have to use the elevator," Mommy said with a sigh.

Hoppity felt a bit scared inside the elevator, but the
elevator operator just smiled and said, "Going up! Which
floor, please?"
Hoppity said loudly, "Toys, please!"

Once inside the Toy Department, Hoppity ran straight for the shelves of small bears. "Look, Tufty!" he said. "Here are some of your cousins!"

Mommy waited patiently until Tufty had been properly introduced to his bear cousins. Then she said, "That's enough. Be a good boy, Hoppity, and leave the bears. You can have just one ride in the racing car."

Hoppity fit perfectly in the racing car. With his feet on the pedals and his hands on the steering wheel, he felt like a professional racing driver.

''I won't be a cymbal-clasher when I'm big,'' he cried. ''I'll be a racing driver!''

''We'll see,'' said Mommy. ''Climb out now!''

As they were leaving the Toy Department, Hoppity was given a big yellow balloon. Before he could thank the kind lady, a voice, as if from nowhere, boomed out, "Special sale on hats and bonnets on the first floor!"

The voice made Hoppity jump. "Where is it?" he whispered. "I can't see where it's coming from!"

"From that loudspeaker on the wall," said Mommy.

Hoppity was still thinking about the magic voice when Mommy went up to the hat counter. Then she met one of her friends and they were soon picking up and trying on bonnets. In the excitement of finding a bargain, she forgot about Hoppity, and soon he wandered away.

"It's time I found something to buy for you, Tufty," he said. And he went over to a basket filled with bright knitted hats and scarves. But finding a hat that fit Tufty's small head was not easy. Hoppity soon began talking just like his mother. "No, not that one—it doesn't suit you . . ." Then something dreadful happened. His beautiful new balloon was suddenly floating away. "Help! Help! Catch it, somebody!" he screamed.

Tufty's present was forgotten as Hoppity chased after the balloon. Soon he was caught up in a crowd of eager shoppers. Then he was swept away. The balloon was lost! Hoppity was lost! And he began to cry. After what seemed like hours, he found himself back in the Shoe Department.

"I'm l-lost!" Hoppity sobbed, when the pretty salesperson came up to him. "I've lost M-Mommy!"

"Don't cry," said the pretty lady, as she helped Hoppity blow his nose on his new handkerchief. "We can find lost Mommies. But first I'll take you to the manager's office."

"My balloon is lost too," Hoppity whispered.

"We'll be happy to find you another one," said the lady.

When the manager told Hoppity he would call his mother over the loudspeaker, Hoppity began to smile. "You must be the magic voice," he said.

"That's right," said the manager. "It's the magic voice that finds lost Mommies." And soon—there was Mommy, very pretty in her new bonnet, hugging and kissing him.

"Why don't you leave Hoppity with us," said the manager, "while you finish shopping?"

Mommy looked doubtful. But then the door opened and in came two more, tearful children. "Don't worry about me," said Hoppity. "I'll tell them all about the magic voice that finds lost Mommies and Daddies."

No wonder Mommy looked so proud as she hurried off!

When they were home again, Mommy went to the mirror to admire her new bonnet. Hoppity showed Daddy his new balloon and Tufty's new hat and all the presents—except the slippers hidden behind the cushion. But most of all he enjoyed telling him about the magic voice that found lost Mommies!

# the New Baby

Tippu and his friend Monty were playing a game in the garden when Mommy appeared. She was pushing the carriage with Tippu's new baby sister in it. "All that noise!" she cried. "I'm afraid the baby will wake up."

Tippu scowled. "That baby spoils everything!" he muttered. But Mommy pretended not to hear.

"I won't be far away," she went on. "Just in the kitchen. But since it's such a nice day, I'm leaving the baby in the garden. So no more noisy games, Tippu—and if your little sister wakes up, come and tell me at once."

"You can't have any fun with a new baby around," grumbled Tippu, as his mother went indoors.

That night, while Mommy was busy ironing, Tippu asked what they were going to do on the first day of his school vacation. "You always take me somewhere special," he said.

"Not this time," said Mommy. "You know we can't leave the baby on her own—" She stopped as Tippu's little sister began crying in the next room. "She must need to be changed," said Mommy. "Be a good boy and sort out the ironing for me while I tend to her."

On Saturday Tippu went to the playground to meet Monty. He was surprised to find that Monty had brought along his little sister. "What a nuisance!" he exclaimed. "Can't you take her home? Then we could have some real fun on our own."

"Of course not," said Monty. "Besides, I like her."

"Please yourself," said Tippu crossly. "My baby sister is just a nuisance. I'll never like her!"

"Oh yes you will," said Monty. "You'll see!" Tippu refused to play with Monty and his sister. But he soon found it wasn't much fun whizzing down the slide all by himself.

Tippu always went roller-skating with Daddy on Saturday afternoons. Daddy liked him in his old play-clothes and didn't mind if his hair was untidy. "That baby can't spoil my roller-skating," Tippu told himself, as he went to tell Daddy he was ready.

"Sorry Tippu, no roller-skating today," said Daddy. "Your Great Aunt Lucy is coming all the way from East Woods with a present for your baby sister. And she will want to see you, too."

But Tippu wasn't there when his Great Aunt Lucy arrived.
She climbed out of her car with the presents, and Tippu's
Mommy and Daddy went to meet her. "I just can't wait to
see the new baby," she cried. "I suppose she's beautiful."
"She is," said Mommy. "We are both thrilled."
"She's just like her mother," said Daddy proudly.

"Where's my Tippu?" Great Aunt Lucy asked as they went indoors. "I have a present for him, too. I thought he would be here to welcome me."

"Oh, he's brushing his hair and making himself tidy for your visit," said Mommy.

"I want to see him first," said Great Aunt Lucy.

But Tippu didn't appear. "We had better look for him," said Great Aunt Lucy. "Perhaps he's playing hide and seek?"

Daddy looked in the kitchen and in the playroom. Then he went outside and looked all around the garden and in the shed. But Tippu was nowhere to be seen.

"I can't find him anywhere," Daddy said at last. Mommy began to look worried.

"Where can he be?" she said. "Why is he hiding from us?"

"Perhaps neither of you have been making a fuss over him since the new baby arrived," suggested Great Aunt Lucy.

Mommy's eyes filled with tears.

The new baby was forgotten until, suddenly, they heard her crying. "She's in her crib upstairs," Daddy said. "I'll tend to her while you look for Tippu." He couldn't believe his eyes when he peeked around the door and saw Tippu!

"Stop crying," Tippu was saying. "I'm here. I'll take care of you." Daddy saw Tippu smile happily as his little sister stopped crying and smiled back at him. "Maybe Monty was right," Daddy heard him say. "I think I could like you, after all!"

Daddy crept downstairs. There was Great Aunt Lucy emptying out the closet hoping she would find Tippu hiding there. "He's upstairs with his baby sister," said Daddy. "He must have been hiding under our bed for most of the time."

"I'll go get him at once," Mommy cried joyfully. "I was beginning to think we had lost our precious Tippu forever!"

When Mommy went into the bedroom Tippu was looking pleased with himself. ''I told her to go to sleep and she did,'' he said.

Mommy began hugging and kissing him. ''Never mind the baby right now,'' she whispered. ''My little boy matters too.''

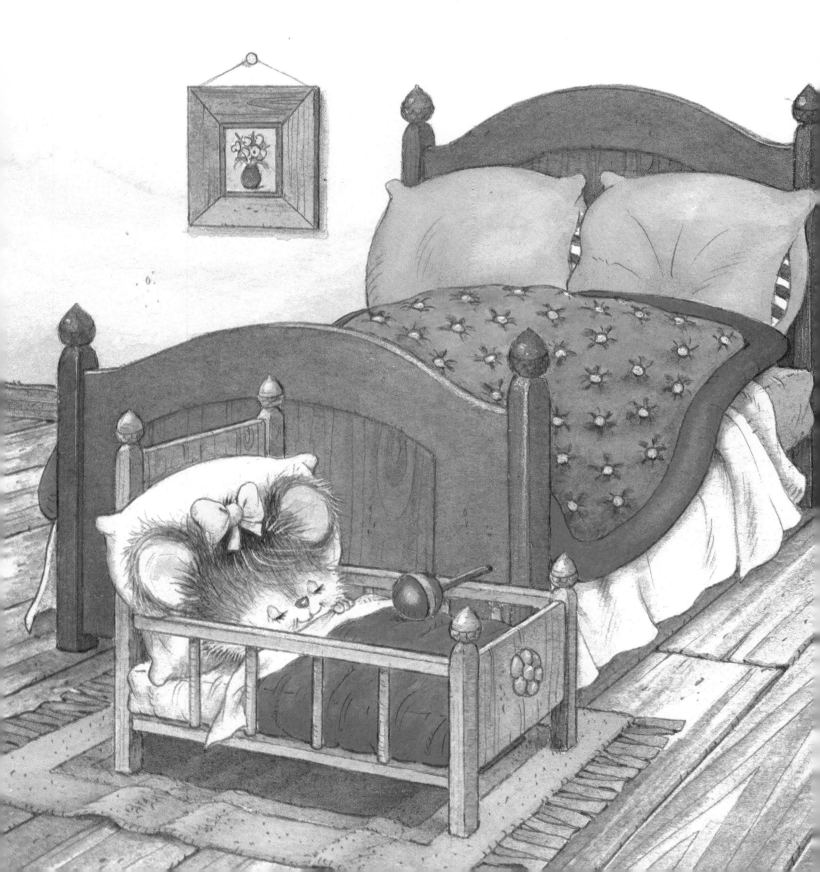

"I-I thought you loved the new baby more than me," Tippu whispered at last.

"How could you think that?" Mommy said softly. "We love you more than ever. It's just that our baby is so new and helpless."

After Great Aunt Lucy had had her tea, Tippu helped her open the presents. There was a brand-new toy car for him and a pretty hat for the baby. "Let me put her new hat on," Tippu cried. And Great Aunt Lucy nodded.

"What a lucky baby she is to have you to take care of her."

"I suppose she is!" said Tippu, as he smiled.

# First Day at School

One morning Chippy went shopping with his mother. He soon found a box of his favorite cereal. But Mommy said, "Put it back, Chippy. We do not need that today."

Chippy was very surprised when he heard his mother ask Mr. Acorn where he kept the workbooks, pencils and crayons.

"At the far end of the store," said Mr. Acorn, smiling.

"Well, well, I suppose you're getting Chippy ready for his first day at school!"

"I don't want to go to school," Chippy said, as they left the store. "I don't want pencils and crayons and workbooks. I want potato chips and some of Mr. Acorn's candy."

Mommy shook her head as she hurried along. "You know it won't be long before you go to school," she said. "And you will need all these things." But Chippy still looked angry and upset as he followed Mommy indoors and watched her put the things she had bought for school in the big chest in her bedroom.

The next day Chippy was riding his tricycle in the garden when his friend, Susie, came along. "Can you come and play?" Chippy asked. "Mommy is too busy to take me out."

Susie hesitated. "I could," she said at last. "But not for long. My Mommy is taking me shopping to get a new dress for my first day at school."

Chippy made a face. "I'm going to hate my first day at school," he said. "Anyway, let's go into the house. Mommy is in the backyard so we can play by ourselves. I've got something to show you."

Chippy took Susie upstairs. "I'll show you what's inside the big chest in Mommy's room," he said. "Follow me!"
Susie helped Chippy raise the heavy lid. Then she gasped.
"All these things are for your first day at school, Chippy!" she cried.
"I guess so," said Chippy. Then he took the new workbook and began tearing out the pages.

Chippy and Susie were having a good time drawing funny faces on the torn out pages of the workbook when Mommy found them. No wonder she was angry! ''You will just have to take your ruined workbook to school,'' she told Chippy.

The very next Monday Chippy left for school. He wore his
new striped T-shirt and he had a new school bag and a big
blue lunch box which was a surprise from Daddy. "I wish
you looked happier," said Mommy, as she hurried him along.

Susie was standing beside the teacher when they arrived.
And Mommy said quickly, "I'll leave you now . . ."

Poor Chippy! He looked so miserable that the teacher called
out, "Come and stand by me, Chippy! You can ring the
school bell."

"I-I don't want to," said Chippy in his sulky voice.

"I do, I do!" Susie cried. "I want to . . ."

"No, you don't," said Chippy. "I'll ring the bell." And he took the big bell and swung it up and down.

"Well done, Chippy," said the teacher, smiling.

It had been fun ringing the big bell. But once inside the classroom, Chippy began to feel miserable again. When the teacher gathered the others around her to listen to a story, Chippy refused to join in. And when he turned his back on her, she pretended not to notice.

But Chippy couldn't help hearing the story and, at last, ever so slowly, he moved towards the others. Soon the teacher was asking, "Who knows what happened next?"

"I know!" said Chippy. "Old Grunter fell over." Everybody clapped and the teacher said, "Very good, Chippy."

"You were clever about the story," Susie whispered, when they sat down to their morning snack. Chippy laughed. Then he opened his brand-new lunch box and found his favorite cookies.

To Susie's surprise, when the teacher asked someone to sweep up the crumbs, Chippy put up his hand. "I thought you hated school," she said softly.

"Oh—well—now I feel different," Chippy murmured. "I just wish I hadn't ruined my workbook."

The teacher was very understanding when she saw what Chippy had done to his workbook. She used her scissors to cut away the torn pages. Then Chippy told her about never wanting his first day at school to happen.

"It's always wise to find out about things first, Chippy," she said, "before you tell yourself you are going to hate them."

And Chippy said, "I hated rice pudding before I first tasted it, but now I like it. So maybe it's just the same with school!" And he smiled happily.